Houndsley and Catina

James Howe

illustrated by Marie-Louise Gay

CANDLEWICK PRESS
CAMBRIDGE, MASSACHUSETTS

for Amelia Englund Keller

J. H.

Text copyright © 2006 by James Howe
Illustrations copyright © 2006 by Marie-Louise Gay

First paperback edition 2007

The Library of Congress has cataloged the hardcover edition as follows:
Howe, James, date.
Houndsley and Catina / James Howe ; illustrated by Marie-Louise Gay. — 1st ed.
p.   cm.
Summary: Houndsley and Catina run into trouble when they decide
to prove that they are the best at cooking and writing, respectively.
ISBN 978-0-7636-2404-0 (hardcover)
[1. Dogs—Fiction. 2. Cats—Fiction. 3. Friendship—Fiction.]
I. Gay, Marie-Louise, ill. II. Title.
PZ7.H83727Hou 2006
[E]—dc22   2005050187

ISBN 978-0-7636-3293-9 (paperback)

2 4 6 8 10 9 7 5 3 1

Printed in Singapore

This book was typeset in Galliard and Tree-Boxelder.
The illustrations were done in watercolor, pencil, and collage.

Candlewick Press
2067 Massachusetts Avenue
Cambridge, Massachusetts 02140

visit us at www.candlewick.com

Contents

Chapter One
The Writer

Catina wanted to be a writer.

Every evening after dinner, she would make herself a cup of ginger tea and sit down to write another chapter in her book.

So far she had written seventy-three chapters.

The book was called *Life Through the Eyes of a Cat*.

"My book will win prizes," Catina told her best friend, Houndsley, one day when he asked how the writing was going.

"I did not ask if your book was going to win prizes," Houndsley said in his soft-as-a-rose-petal voice. "I asked how the writing was going."

"I will be famous," Catina went on as if she had not heard him.

Houndsley sighed. "May I read your book?" he asked.

"Of course," said Catina. "I have only one chapter left to write."

The next evening, Catina invited Houndsley to her house.

"Here is my book," she said proudly.
She gave him all seventy-four chapters, a
cup of ginger tea, and a plate of cookies.

"I will need more cookies," said
Houndsley.

Catina did not take her eyes off
Houndsley while he read. He wished the
phone would ring so she would have to
go to another room.

Here is some of what Houndsley read:

On the subject of mice,
enough cannot ~~bee~~ be said.
But who am I to say?

I have known many mice
in my life. They are all
right. For rodents.
Well, I am bored
writing ~~abut~~ about mice.
Who cares, anyway?

Oh, dear, Houndsley thought. *Catina is a terrible writer. What am I going to say to her?*

"I am at a loss for words," Houndsley told Catina when he had finished reading the book. "I am speechless."

Catina beamed. "My writing has left you speechless?" she exclaimed. "Now I know I will be a famous writer! Oh, thank you, Houndsley!"

"You're welcome," Houndsley said.

But he was thinking, *Oh, dear. Poor Catina.*

Chapter Two
Cooking Contest

Every Saturday night, Houndsley cooked dinner for his best friend, Catina, and his next-door neighbor Bert.

This was not always easy. Even though she was a cat, Catina did not eat meat. And what Bert liked best were seeds, grains, and worms.

But Houndsley did not mind. He enjoyed cooking. And he was good at it.

One Saturday night, Bert said, "Everything you make is delicious, Houndsley. I've never had worms with poppy seeds and broccoli before."

"Worms?!" Catina yelped. "You know I'm a vegetarian!"

"They are not real worms," Houndsley assured his friend. "They only look like worms. They are made of tofu."

Catina laughed. "You are a wonder," she said.

"Yes," said Bert. "You should enter the cooking contest."

"Cooking contest? Oh, I don't know about that," Houndsley said, his voice growing softer with each word.

"But you are a great cook!" Catina cried. "You could be famous!"

"Do you think so?" Houndsley asked.

"I know so!" said Catina. "When you have a talent as big as yours, you must share it with the world!"

"Really?"

"First prize is a set of pots and pans,"

said Bert.

"I could use a new set of pots and pans," said Houndsley, although he already had so many he was not sure where he would put them. "All right, I will do it!"

On the day of the cooking contest,
Houndsley arrived with everything
he needed.

"I am going to make my three-bean chili," Houndsley told Catina and Bert, who had come to cheer him on.

"Your three-bean chili is delicious," Catina told him. "You will win."

Houndsley blushed. He thought he might win, too, but he did not dare to say so.

"I did not know so many others would be here," Houndsley said.

"Look, Houndsley," said Bert. "You are going to be on television!"

Oh, dear, Houndsley thought.

Everyone will be watching me.

Houndsley had made his three-bean
chili many times before, but today
everything went wrong.

He dropped a can of tomatoes on
his foot.

He did not cook the rice long enough.

And he forgot to put in the beans.

All three kinds!

When the judges came to taste his chili, they made faces.

"I think I broke a tooth on the rice," one of them said.

"I don't taste the beans," said another.

"Maybe you should call this no-bean chili," said a third, and all the judges laughed.

Houndsley had never been so embarrassed in his life.

"I will never cook again," he told Catina and Bert.

"Not even for us?" Bert said.

"Maybe for you," said Houndsley. "But please do not ask for three-bean chili."

Chapter Three
fireflies

One night, Houndsley and Catina were

sitting outside watching fireflies. This was

one of their favorite things to do together.

They sat quietly for a long time.

At last, Houndsley said, "I did not need a new set of pots and pans. I only wanted to win that contest to show everyone I was the best cook."

"You are the best cook," Catina said.

"I do not need to be the best," said Houndsley in his soft-as-a-rose-petal voice. "I just enjoy cooking. Trying to be the best made me nervous, and I did not have fun. If you do not have fun doing something you like to do, what is the point?"

Catina thought about this.

"I do not have fun writing," she said
as they began to walk. "My mind wanders
and I get bored."

A firefly blinked at her.

"I want to be a famous writer," she went on, "but I do not like to write."

"Perhaps you will be famous at something else," said Houndsley.

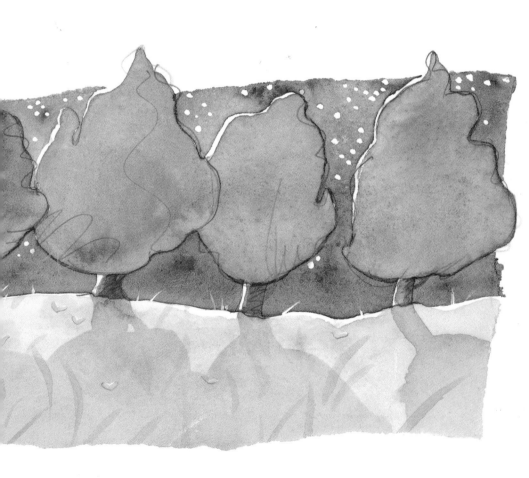

"Yes," Catina said. "First I will find something I like to do. Then I will do it and do it and do it until I am very good at it. And then I might be famous."

"I know something you are good at already," said Houndsley, "although you will never be famous for it."

"What?"

"Being my friend."

Catina began to purr. "Being your friend is better than being famous," she said.

Houndsley and Catina came to their favorite spot. They sat for a long time. They did not talk about winning prizes or being famous. They did not talk about anything. They smelled the sweet summer air and listened to crickets. They watched the fireflies dance and blink and light up the night in front of them.

Everyone has talents. Watching fireflies was one of theirs.